Kafka Kafka

docufictions

Harold Jaffe

SPUYTEN DUYVIL
New York City

Gratitude to Sebastian Bennett, Robert Cross, Tom Whalen, and Joan Raymond for commenting on this volume in manuscript.

for those artists who have forged
beauty out of extreme emotional pain

PANTHER

Distinguished members of the Fellowship
You have done me the honor of inviting me to give you an account of the life I formerly led as a ferocious beast of prey.

That is to say, of the transition from my life as a panther of the African savanna to my current life as a human, or species of human.

As a consequence, I am standing here at the podium in my tuxedo and bow tie with my panther's black pelt whitened and my panther's tail tucked into my trousers behind me where you cannot see it.

Please observe that my panther's ferocious claws are gloved and my gleaming fangs are filed, such that if I were to bound from the podium and savage you, I would not rip you apart at once.

Not that I would wish to, you understand.

To rip you apart would mean to partake of your flesh, which, as a reborn human, I have of course forsaken.

Which does not mean that you do not eminently deserve to be ripped apart, savaged, obliterated.

Notwithstanding, I am honored to be invited to join your human fraternity in however provisional a capacity.

And I vow to conduct myself in a humanly manner while recounting to you something of my former life and especially my transit from proud panther to humble human.

I say "former," but it has scarcely been three years since I was shot at for sport on one of your safaris on the African savanna.

I naturally expected to die violently, then be gutted, skinned, mutilated, and mounted on a wall in a hunting lodge or museum, because it is universally known that humans behave in that manner toward all living things, not excluding members of their own species.

Instead I was taken captive.

From my home beneath the limitless sky I was transported by steamship in a stinking, cramped cage where I could scarcely stand, let alone pace.

While caged, the humans—deckhands and such— fulsome in their pride at having captured a black panther, would glower and make faces at me.

They would poke each other in the ribs and laugh and spit at me between the bars of the cage.

Their laughter had always a gruff bark in it that sounded menacing but meant little.

When they talked it was usually about their fantasies of becoming rich and their envy of rich and famous celebrities.

They talked loudly, interchangeably, using the same words and gestures.

They did this not so much intentionally, but as though they simply could not hear how they or their companions actually sounded.

As if their inner ear and brain had lost the capacity to hear and observe.

Lost the capacity or more likely forfeited it.

After observing those humans and others for the length of the voyage, I made the fateful decision that I would be released from captivity.

The release would entail reconstituting myself to look and act human.

This, you must understand, I did not construe as freedom but simply as an expedient, a temporary way out of my predicament.

Not freedom because it became abundantly clear that you self-glorified *Homo sapiens*, rather than employing your natural freedom to remove or even loosen the chains of those less fortunate, were in fact suppressing your own freedom.

And in the process tormenting everything within reach: wilderness, animals, other humans, and whatever residue remained of your sympathetic imaginations.

I say that you tormented everything "within reach," but as you well know and take enormous pride in, with the aid of your revered technology, your imprisoning reach spans and infects the entire globe and beyond into the heavenly regions.

Into the infernal regions as well.

With the aid of technology, your imprisoning reach extends deep into consciousness itself, which it then neutralizes and sanitizes.

For no other reason, it appears, than to suppress the natural play of freedom with which you were gifted.

And, needless to say, to accumulate ever greater power and profit.

My decision to become a species of human, then, had nothing to do with your vaunted freedom but rather with a way out of my immediate predicament.

I will not lie: The other option, just as compelling, was to die, starve myself to death.

I say "just as compelling"; in fact, death made the much greater claim.

Why I chose instead the more degrading option of becoming human, I cannot plausibly explain to you.

I was calculating then as a panther and now, nearly three years later, I am trying to recount that calculation as a human, or species of human.

Perhaps it was simply the challenge, which once conquered, would permit me to display my "humanness," as I am doing here and now in my tuxedo and bow tie, elevated on this podium.

The inescapable fact is that I am still fundamentally a black panther, that fierce and terrifying beast of prey.

That emblem of satanic energy which once you let down your guard will seize you by the throat, snap your spine, drag you under.

I am also, thanks to you, a wounded panther, and it is this deep and grievous wound, obscured by my tuxedo, that I touch with my gloved claw and recall with every dignified word I utter to you, my human brethren.

In truth, the challenge of becoming human was even easier than I had envisioned.

In short order, with very little practice, I taught myself to spit, laugh mockingly, defer absolutely to wealth, talk into my cellular phone while stroking it, surf the Internet, pray.

All the while being blandly complicit in the official ongoing ethnicide throughout the globe of humans unlike me and my kind.

I say "unlike," but the humans you humans exterminate are, to the outside eye, quite like you, except that their skin is darker, they speak another dialect, or they profess to worship a different, though always similar, god.

Regarding my panther-like appearance, cosmetic medical technology excised most of the physical anomalies.

Very expensive procedures, to be sure, the special privilege of the privileged class.

However, my benefactors—impresarios are what they actually are—underwrote the expense with the expectation of realizing a commanding profit from my ongoing "performances."

For my part, I mean to do everything in my power to repay their investment.

Perhaps even in ways they may not have anticipated.

Please observe that I am still large, lithe, unimaginably strong, but that I walk with a stoop to disguise it.

I carry a cane; you can see it beneath me, leaning against the lectern.

I wear spectacles to deflect the furious glare of my eye.

Suppressing my naturally harsh growl, I effect the same deceptively bland voice and homogenous speech patterns that the current crop of upper middle class males possess.

Here I am then, honored members of the Fellowship.

Your guest speaker for the evening.

torque

   sinew
tail-whip   pace-rage
savanna-no-sound
silk-blood-coil
         blood-bang
engine-fury-eye-drill
 sleep-no-sheep moon-grace

pulse-rage

motion   motion

Of course, that was then.

Now I am a gentleman, human like you, honored members of the Fellowship.

Ego-bound.

Brittle.

Infinitely tumored.

terrified of dying.

Pious enemy of wilderness both in and out of consciousness.

Planet despoiler.

I am human, I say, like you, but I am not you.

I am still, in the deepest recesses, a panther.

My articulate tucked-in tail confirms it.

My just-contained restraint which prevents me from pouncing from the podium and savaging you, attests to it.

My connection to the immemorial pulse of the African savanna testifies to it.

August members of the Fellowship, I thank you yet again for courteously inviting me to present an account of the transition from panther to human.

This will be the last time I thank you.

It is poor form for humans of your rank to be thanked overmuch.

Truly, I owe you an inestimable debt which even now—at this moment—I am devising to repay in kind.

I trust you have been duly entertained.

Country Doctor

The summons came at 4:50 AM. It was "urgent."

A child was perilously ill in the tiny hamlet of Achtal, some 14 miles from my home-office in Lichteneck.

It was dark with an icy drizzle, my car was unreliable, and my eyes were far from trustworthy in the dark.

I had no choice, I was the district doctor who lived alone.

I did have an elderly helper but he was in Vienna for a funeral and not expected back for several days.

I myself was elderly and had served as a doctor in the same district for 36 years.

I warmed up some tea which I sipped rapidly. I bit into a stale roll which I then packed in a small bag to take with me.

Bundled up against the cold, I cursorily checked my doctor's case, then climbed into the small car.

It was dark and foggy with a cold drizzle and the defroster was broken but I had been to Achtal many times and depended for the most part on "muscle memory."

Strangely, no sooner had I started the engine than I was there outside the small cottage in Achtal which I could see in the dawn light was filled with family and probably neighbors, though the area itself was mostly desolate, enveloped by the deep woods of the Kobernauser Wald.

Ash, beech, oak, pine, spruce, fir, larch.

A large woman, deeply worried, followed by a teenage girl, probably her daughter, nodded to me with her hands clasped while I was still in my car looking for a dry spot to park.

A very large man, evidently the husband, took my doctor's case and led me immediately into the sickroom which was very small and airless, almost unbreathable.

The child, a boy of about 8, was sunk deep under rough blankets in his narrow cot.

Someone took my coat while the boy, his child's torso naked, extended his very thin arms and pulled me close to him.

The child's body was clammy with perspiration.

The steam heat in the small room was close to suffocating, nor was I allowed time to open a window.

Without even washing my hands I leaned close to the child's face.

He whispered: "Doctor. Please let me die."

I glanced around the room—only I had heard his whispered plea.

I gazed into the boy's vacant eyes.

I felt his pulse which was normal.

I laid my moist beard on his sunken chest which shivered.

So far as I could tell his heart was normal.

The teenage daughter had moved a small chair into the crowded room for my doctor's case.

I was about to withdraw my stethoscope when the father pushed a glass of brandy at me.

I took a sip and set it on the chair next to my case.

I withdrew the small light from my case and examined the boy's eyes, nose and throat.

His parents and sister as well as apparent neighbors were crowded into the room waiting expectantly for the doctor's verdict.

To their obvious dismay I pronounced the child sound and immediately felt strong arms clasping my chest from behind.

I smelled the father's liquored breath as well as the sweat from his arms.

I squirmed free and as I was closing my case in preparation to leave, I had another look at the boy.

This time I discovered something grave.

The wound just beneath his right hip was raw and pulsating and about as large as my fist.

The open "fist" was rose-red in variations of red, dark in the hollows, lighter at the edges, granulated, with irregular clots of blood which were oozing pus. * The child's neck glands were badly swollen.

That was how it looked from a short distance, but on closer inspection there were still further complications.

I could not suppress a low whistle of astonishment.

In the center of the open fist were maggots, oddly yellow with their pointed conical bodies and blunted posteriors and two dark areas at the pointed end that resemble eyes.

The child heaved himself up so that he had his skeleton arms around my neck, pulling me toward him.

He whispered: "Doctor, save me."

I nodded gently and pulled away while contemplating: Poor boy, you are long past saving; that great blossom in your side is devouring you.

I turned to the family with mournful eyes and they—

all of them, family and friends—were exceedingly pleased.

Excitedly, they stripped me naked and moved me into the main room which was crowded with family and guests.

Collectively, the thirty or so humans in the small house in Achtal, sang at me loudly:

He's a doctor
Strip him naked
If he doesn't cure us kill him, kill him

Someone spat into my ear—I think the mother: "You're not a doctor. A doctor heals."

Someone shouted: "He's a Jew, not a doctor! Look at him!"

Then, still naked, I was forced into the narrow cot with the dying child even as they were hurling insults at me. The dying boy held me with his bony arms so that his teeming wound was flush against my thigh, while they—all of them—sang:

He's a doctor
He's a Jew
Be joyous
He will die naked in bed beside you

But then I was back in my car, still naked, but with my clothes in a heap beside me.

Believe me when I say that even a response as surreally irrational as I describe here is not unusual for a district doctor in the Austrian forest.

Why then do I tolerate it?

I regret to say that a deep and silent wound is all I brought into this world; that is my sole endowment.

*I have taken a few very short passages from Kafka's story.

THE GREAT WALL OF CHINA

Franz Kafka was 26, 10 years before he was diagnosed with tuberculosis; Andrea Ahrens was also 26. Moreover, they were both Jewish and born on the same day, July 3, 1886, in Prague: an irresistible series of coincidences to both of them, especially Kafka.

Kafka and Andrea were lovers who never made love; their vow, initiated by Kafka, was to wait until they walked across the Great Wall of China, from opposite ends, and when they finally met at a small Buddhist temple approximately halfway they would embrace and marry.

Kafka was certain that he had been Chinese in a previous life and though he had never seen it in the live, the Great Wall was often in his dreams and ruminations. As was his wont, Kafka thoroughly researched the project. The Great Wall began construction in 221 BCE, continued for more than 2300 years and is estimated to be 13,171 miles (21,196 kilometers) long. The primary motive of the construction was to protect China from violent nomads to the north and west. However, because of necessity the massive wall was constructed unevenly, with gaps, hence invaders such as Genghis Khan's Mongols were able to successfully breach the fortifications.

As Kafka sketched out his grand idea, Andrea would start her journey at Shai Hai Guan, on the shores of the Yellow Sea, walking westward, whereas K would start at Jai Yu Guan, the southwestern periphery of the Gobi Desert, walking eastward. They would finally meet after approximately 90 days of medium-paced walking at the Baoguang Buddhist Temple, which K estimated to be in the middle of their journey.

Regarding the construction of the Wall, which took nearly two and a half centuries, it had to be built piecemeal. As Kafka put it in his notes: Because of the length of the Wall most of the "masons" were amateurs, and they could not be expected to "lay one stone on another for years on end in an uninhabited mountainous region, hundreds of miles from their homes . . . It was for this reason that the system of piecemeal building was instituted. Five hundred yards in five years was the general rule," after which the masons were presented with official badges of honor.

Piecemeal construction by amateur masons, however conscientious, resulted in an unevenness in construction with occasional gaps in the Wall itself. If the Chinese were so concerned with nomadic invasion why didn't they make a point of filling in the gaps? To this question, Kafka provides a curious response: "We Chinese possess certain folk and political institutions that are unique in their clarity, others again unique in their obscurity. And the construction of the Wall is essentially involved with each of these traits, especially the obscurity."

Kafka continues: Clearly the piecemeal construction of the Great Wall was—or should have been—makeshift, provisional. "Blocks of wall left standing in deserted regions could be easily pulled down again and again by the nomads." Why then did the high command, with its anxiety about violent intrusion, insist on an inexpedient construction? In the early days of construction, there was a "secret maxim: Try with all your might to comprehend the decrees of the high command, but only up to a certain point, then avoid further meditation."

Ah, the inscrutable East! And yet Kafka, Chinese in

his previous life, was intent to walk the Great Wall of China

Although I have not yet written specifically about Kafka's partner and "lover" Andrea Ahrens, it should be said that after initial uncertainty, she became nearly as enthusiastic about the majestic art "performance" as Kafka. Like K, Andrea came from a secular Jewish family. Her father was a wealthy importer of artistic goods from China, Korea, and India: Buddhist and Hindu tapestries, sacred objets-d'art, stone figurines... Andrea was fluent in Czech and German, and like Milena Jesenska, K's inamorata a decade later, she was a translator from German to Czech. Andrea had only read three or four of K's writings, but they were enough for her to be convinced of his genius. However, Kafka refused to have them translated from German to Czech (Kafka wrote his fiction in German), and published in a Prague literary journal.

Overall, Andrea did cede to him, though far from absolutely. It was she who, after borrowing money from her resistant father, was in the process of accumulating a year's supply of non-perishable food, lightweight tents, and camping stoves.

Their journey was to be called "The Lovers," and as Max Brod, in his biography of Kafka, put it: "Exhilarated by the emotional and physical scale of their project, the pair imagined themselves walking alone across great expanses of the Chinese landscape, camping under the stars and concluding the journey with love forever."

As suggested, Kafka was almost entirely involved in the, as it were, philosophical aspects of their journey, whereas Andrea paid close attention to the innumerable practical necessities. But neither of them was prepared to confront China's infinite bureaucracy.

Because of the dearth of up-to-date news from distant countries, neither K nor Andrea was aware of what was going on in China. They were preparing to make their journey in 1912, but China had declared itself a republic on January 1, 1912 after the 1911 revolution which overthrew the Qing dynasty, the last imperial dynasty of China. Sun Yat-sen, its founder and provisional president, served only briefly before handing over the presidency to Yuan Shikai, the leader of the Beiyan Army. Yuan rapidly became authoritarian and used his military power to control the administration.

What that meant for "the lovers" was even more

bureaucracy. Kafka actually borrowed money from his sister to make a "fact-finding" trip to Beijing, having managed to enlist the Austrian ambassador to China who agreed to attend Kafka's half-hour-scheduled meeting with high-level bureaucrats and translate Kafka's German to Mandarin.

In short, the Beijing bureaucrats were utterly unaware of what an art performance signified, especially in regard to the Great Wall of China. Kafka explained that the lovers' intention was to sleep on the wall, or if that was prohibited, outside the wall in Chinese homes or hostels, where there were hostels.

Kafka was not at all optimistic about his reception; the best he could get was that the bureaucracy would consider it. His diplomat-translator promised, though without enthusiasm, to raise the issue again. Still, Kafka was not discouraged, which may seem odd, since Kafka is known for his depression and skepticism. But it is critical to realize that much of the negativity came later, after he was diagnosed with consumption, and toward the end of the Weimar proto-Nazi era when vvirulent anti-Semitism had spread throughout Central Europe.

Meanwhile there was no news from Beijing. When, after six weeks, Kafka wrote to the Austrian ambassador he waited nearly four months to receive a brief reply which said in effect that the diplomat did not yet raise the issue.

Oddly, the disappointment with China negatively affected the relationship between K and Andrea. One might think that the perhaps temporary China disappointment would bring the "lovers" together, but it produced the opposite. They met occasionally briefly, never spoke about marriage, and rarely embraced.

Meanwhile Kafka waited another three months before writing the Austrian ambassador again. This time the reply came in a fortnight. It was brief:

"Herr Kafka: China's response to your 'performance' idea is a conclusive No. Best not to pursue the idea."

**

Interestingly, the Serbian performance artist Maria Abramovic and her long-time German partner Ulay redeemed Kafka and Andrea's abortive trip in 1988. Their performance was also called The Lovers, with the intention of meeting halfway at a temple and marrying. And they too ran into extreme bureaucratic difficulties which delayed their performance by six years. By the time they met after 90 arduous days trekking their attitude to each other had altered entirely and they decided mutually not to marry but to break up. They did not see each other for more than 20 years, soon after which Ulay died. (Neither Abramovic nor Ulay seemed to be aware of Kafka and Andrea's thwarted trip 70 years earlier.)

WHITE FOOD

Under a photo of processed cheese, ham, and crackers packed neatly in plastic, a Chinese microblogger writes that to eat this for lunch is to "learn what it feels like to be dead."

The post is part of a trend among Chinese social media users who are recreating "báirén fàn" or "white people food" to better understand western packed lunches made up of plain ingredients such as raw vegetables and sliced meats. The social media platforms Weibo and Xiaohongshu have been inundated with photos and reviews of cold sandwiches, raw carrots and canned tuna. Many are from Chinese students perplexed by the banal lunches eaten by their peers overseas.

Chinese people in Europe have shared similar assessments, with one Chinese in Switzerland saying they have a colleague whose lunch has not changed for 10 years. "It is a fistful of oatmeal mixed with low-fat yogurt, with half an apple and a carrot. If such a meal is to extend life, what is the meaning of life?"

CLOUD STAR

His gift was to mount the face of skyscrapers or "towers" without the use of apparatus. Just his small hands and small prehensile-like feet. His body was slight, though well-made and extraordinarily flexible, not through elaborate preparation and exercise, but naturally. He was 15 years old and orphaned, so there was no way of establishing whether his gift was transmitted though his family.

Like virtually every artist in these broken days, he had an agent, or manager, who looked after his every need. The boy, called Cloud, was uncommonly sensitive, even delicate—despite his athletic gifts. Except for his manager who loved him like a son, he had no friends and no family, just admirers.

On a Saturday or Sunday dusk when the June weather was still light and relatively calm Cloud would perform his well-publicized climb on the face of a building— virtually any building, even one 40 stories high and seemingly smooth as a mirror with no visible footholds.

Moreover, Cloud climbed rapidly: making his way up a smooth "tower" 40 floors high would commonly take Cloud less than two hours. And he wouldn't be winded.

Once on the roof, Cloud would retreat into small temporary living quarters that were prearranged for him, and he would be given food and drink for sustenance. Customarily he would drink distilled water or fresh cherry juice and eat nut butter spooned from a bowl. Rarely anything else.

Although Cloud was becoming well-known—even famous—he preferred to climb in the same area of the large city and reside—if that is the correct term— in familiar quarters on familiar roofs. The problem was that with his burgeoning fame on social media Cloud's abilities were always desired elsewhere. Which naturally meant more money, which naturally mattered to Cloud's manager, though not in the least to the boy.

Making matters more complicated was Cloud's' refusal to fly. Air travel horrified him, so that when, reluctantly, he accepted a proposal to perform on another giant tower in another large city, he and his manager would travel in the early morning by fast train in a private compartment. Where there was only bus travel available Cloud would simply refuse to go.

Once, en route to Philadelphia, three hours to the west, Cloud was reclining on the luggage rack as was his habit, while his manager was sitting across from him scrolling through his mobile. Suddenly the manager heard a gasp, as though an intake of breath. Immediately he stood and put his face close to Cloud, who appeared to be weeping.

"Come closer," Cloud whispered between sobs.

"What is it, my genius?" Cloud's manager whispered tenderly.

"There must be a change," Cloud whispered. "At once."

"A change?"

"I must have a companion. A female. Someone to reside with me on the rooftops."

After a difficult moment, the manager whispered: "Do you mean to get married, my young friend?"

"I don't know. I just want someone to reside with me on the rooftops or else I will not be able to continue."

"I will do what I can, my beautiful boy."

After this grievous conversation, Cloud experienced some difficulty climbing the face of the tower in Philadelphia. Once a misplaced toehold had him swinging from the 27th story by his fingertips—but he recovered to the wild applause of the onlookers, most of whom assumed it was a deliberate flourish.

The manager, however, recognized that he must act immediately. Instead of putting an ad on social media and receiving thousands of responses, he phoned several other managers and in short order settled on a 16-year-old rock climber.

Her performance name was Star, and she was introduced to Cloud on a roof of a Pittsburgh tower he had just climbed and nearly lost his footing again. Cloud's manager crossed his fingers, but the good news was that they took to each other at once. Star was waiting in the tiny apartment on the roof when Cloud, uncommonly out of breath, was introduced to her by her manager. As they embraced—two sweet-faced teens—Star and Cloud's managers shook hands.

So that potentially disastrous hurdle was overcome. Then something unexpected occurred: Star, the rock climber, decided she wished to climb the faces of towers even as her lover (yes, they became lovers) did. Already a famous rock climber for her age, she rapidly became an adept tower climber under Cloud's scrupulous tutelage.

Tutoring Star while himself performing (and making love in his off-hours) seemed to tire Cloud. His manager, familiar with Cloud's technique could see it, and it worried him. However, he did not know quite what to do about it. Were he to caution Cloud to get his rest (which naturally would be more than before Star), the boy would not respond well.

Meanwhile Star was making such rapid progress that she and Cloud began climbing towers together, usually in tandem. It seemed to Cloud's manager that the boy was intent on refining his lover's skill until she was his equal. That prospect worried Cloud's manager, but delighted Star's manager because the already large audience nearly doubled and the money was pouring in.

For his part, Cloud seemed contented, though often tired from the loving attention he paid to Star. As Cloud's manager viewed it, Cloud seemed intent on developing Star to become his equal—even superior. And by degree, Star, a year older than Cloud, became dominant both as lover and climber.

Publicly, the tandem of two barefoot, teenaged child-faced tower climbers was an enormous success and championed by everyone except Cloud's manager who harbored feelings of doubt, even dread. Meanwhile, Cloud, who previously loved his manager like a father, was drawing farther away from him into the orbit of Star.

When the troupe of Cloud, Star, and their two managers traveled by fast train, Cloud no longer settled himself on the luggage rack but sat next to Star on the compartment seats facing the two managers. The four made a longer-than-usual trip to Boston which was further held up because of some sort of engine difficulty.

The 60-floor all-glass Hancock Tower in Boston, never climbed before, was their destination, and the tandem climb was scheduled for 7:00 PM, Saturday, when the July evening was still light and the weather was cool. Instead of having his customary nap after a longish journey, Cloud spent his time with Star in their hotel room examining the blueprints of Hancock Tower and presumably making love.

Instead of Cloud leading the way with Star a floor behind, that was reversed with Star ascendant and Cloud behind: two beautiful barefoot children. By the time they had reached the 15th story they had established their pace. Later, at the 37th floor, they decided to try something they had done in practice trials. Pulling abreast of each other they held hands while clinging to the tower one-handedly.

Suddenly, the clouds darkened and in a flinch it was raining heavily.

Then one of them was falling head-first. It was Star who fell to her death, after which Cloud's grip slipped— or he let go—and he too fell. Both were dead and the spectacle was over.

However, it wasn't over on social media, where conspiracy went viral: *The two climbers were at odds; Star was made pregnant by Cloud's manager; Cloud deliberately let go of Star's hand, then himself fell deliberately.* Those and kindred rumors spread madly until they were overtaken by fresher spectacles, such as teens in bikinis jumping from helicopters without parachutes and landing on their skateboards.

TASTE OF CHERRY

Kwanted to kill himself, shoot himself in the left temple.

But he didn't want to do it himself.

Why not?

That's a bit complicated: He seemed to feel that if he killed himself it would possibly be sinful, but if someone else put the .38 to his left temple and blasted him, maybe he wouldn't go to hades or whatever is down there.

That sounds stupid and K wasn't stupid.

It could be that his actual fear was that if he were to hold the .38 to his left temple he might jerk it away at the last second and possibly incapacitate himself without killing himself.

He had the .38, unregistered, purchased from a friend now dead who built firearms, so there wouldn't be a problem on that side.

And he had 30 thousand dollars to give to the human who pulled the trigger.

The question was locating that human.

He didn't want it to be someone he was close to or knew well because he didn't want them to try to talk him out of it.

Nor did he want them to worry or grieve.

It was his business, his terminal disgust with the world, especially his self-disgust for being so useless and impotent in a world gone crazy.

He'd try Drew, a man about his age, widower, childless, Vietnam vet, first lieutenant in the infantry, who knew how to fire a handgun.

Drew lived alone, didn't have much money, and felt isolated.

K and Drew had met eight or nine years ago in AA, but rarely saw each other anymore.

Every other year or so they'd exchange Xmas cards.

He emailed Drew and arranged a meeting at a public library that both of them occasionally visited.

The first appointed meeting didn't work because Drew said he forgot about it.

The second meeting ten days later worked.

K and Drew, each in their pandemic masks, talked quietly in the reading room, and when K made his pitch about wanting to be killed and how the gun would be untraceable and especially the 30 thousand dollars, Drew just looked at him.

After maybe two minutes of staring at him over his mask with a look of—what?—pity, surprise, disappointment, Drew quietly said: No, got up and walked out of the library.

K had the loaded .38 in his car.

He returned to his apartment, shook out the rounds from the pistol, then lay down on his back.

He dreamt.

He was driving an inadequate American-made sedan in perilous terrain and became lost.

Mountainous, with steep peaks and bottomless abysses, he was it seemed, in Dante's Inferno.

He drove carefully down a path and consulted a human who suddenly appeared.

The man looked K up and down with a scornful glare.

K drove away abruptly, but when he nearly drove off the uneven path into an abyss, he began to back up awkwardly, he wasn't sure in which direction.

Unexpectedly, someone called Virgil, stepped out of a hut.

Virgil, calmly, with a neutral look, commenced to lead K back out of the Inferno.

Later that evening K emailed Mia, a sort of informal physical therapist he worked with five or six years ago after his left hip replacement.

They got along easily, but after Mia lost her physical therapy job, they lost touch.

The last K knew Mia was cleaning house to keep up.

He remembered that she lived with her newly divorced daughter.

Mia agreed to meet with him three days later after work—she was still cleaning house.

They met at a small café.

Mia looked weary; she ordered a no-frills coffee.

—You look good, K. Are you still writing?

—Still at it, Mia.

K suddenly remembered her daughter's name.

—How is Angel? Is she still living with you?

—Yes. She's not well, K. She was diagnosed with

breast cancer. She's undergoing tests now to see whether the cancer has spread into her lymph nodes.

K looked at Mia who had her head bowed.

—Can I ask you, Mia, whether you are okay with money?

—Well, she has health insurance, but it doesn't seem to cover all of it. You know how it is.

—Let me help you, Mia. I'll write you a check right now.

—Oh, K. That's kind of you, but, honestly, I don't know when I can pay you back.

—Please don't worry about that, Mia.

K wrote Mia a check for five thousand dollars.

He didn't have the heart to ask about the suicide venture.

That evening K began to write a fiction loosely based on the 1997 Iranian film called "Taste of Cherry."

The director, Abbas Kiarostami, exiled in Paris, had just died.

K wrote for several hours, then slept fitfully, with one dream piggybacking another.

The dream he remembered when he woke early in

the morning had to do with giving a ten-dollar bill to a homeless Black man spread on his back in front of Walmart.

The man took hold of K's hand and wouldn't let go.

Despite the pandemic and the fact that the homeless man was maskless and possibly contagious, K held on to his hand.

That dream gave him the idea of enlisting someone down on his luck that K did not know.

The person would have to be intact enough to pull the trigger without misfiring.

Despite edicts and penalties, homeless people were camped all over the city.

K, with his loaded revolver and 25 thousand dollars, drove south to Island Street where there were numerous encampments.

He parked his car and walked for several blocks, reminded of fractured India where he spent time on a fellowship many years ago.

He gave five and ten dollar bills to several homeless, but nobody seemed quite right for his alter-suicide.

The next day at approximately the same time he did

it again, beginning from a different street in the same area.

This time he was stopped by a homeless white man, dark-complexioned.

The man slipped on his mask and he and K walked.

Oddly, he said his name was Krishna, but he was built more like Ganesh, Lord Shiva's son, the elephant God, with a burly chest.

K wondered how Krishna could be homeless and still hefty.

They talked.

Krishna claimed he was an army veteran of the Gulf War in the early 1990s, but was laid off his construction job several months ago and was living on the streets.

They walked quietly then stopped in front of a satellite Apple store.

Youthful tech-humans glided in and out.

K and Krishna paused under a withered sycamore.

K asked the fellow whether he was familiar with firearms and Krishna said he was.

Then K put it to him: He knew a mostly deserted desert-like area east of the city which was easy to find and get to by bus.

K drew Krishna a simple map.

They would meet at 7 pm, the next day after the sun set.

K would give Krishna 10 thousand dollars and the loaded .38.

After killing K, Krishna would find a card in K's left trouser pocket specifying where the other 15 thousand dollars were hidden.

Krishna did not seem surprised at the strange offer, nor did he ask questions.

They parted.

At home, K had little to do.

Dido, his sweet cat, died a year ago, so there was no longer an animal to look after.

He had published books and manuscripts in his rented house but didn't care what happened to them.

He had friends and several acquaintances but wouldn't contact them.

K drove to the appointed spot early and Krishna was already there.

K locked his car and took the key.

Krishna followed K for 50 yards or so into a more deserted area.

They stopped.

—Are you ready, Krishna?

—Yes.

K gave Krishna the 10 thousand dollars in a sealed envelope which Krishna slipped into his pocket.

K pointed to his pocket where the index card with the map of the other 15 thousand was.

K then gave him the loaded pistol.

Krishna opened the cylinder, spun it, then closed it.

As K turned sideways so that his left temple was targeted, Krishna turned without a word and ran in the opposite direction, dropping the pistol en route.

K turned to watch him run fast without turning.

After a short time K drove home without his loaded pistol and 10 thousand dollars.

He took a plastic bottle of water out of the fridge, turned on his computer and resumed writing the fiction he called "Taste of Cherry."

BURROW

All my life I've wanted to live underground and have fantasized repeatedly about my own burrow. It would naturally be in the country—what's left of it—and it would be intricately constructed because of climate and predation. I am a predator myself of course but am older now and naturally need to be more cautious.

I say "older now" but I've lived my life as a hunter and still hunt, though not nearly as daringly as when I was younger. I've had many close calls but have always managed to elude capture and the inevitable cannibalism. However, I am not nearly as supple, my reflexes are not as quick. As a result my burrow is as advantageously constructed as I could manage. It contains 11 units plus a large main unit which I call the keep, as in castle keep. It is there that I keep most— though not all—of the booty. Several of the small units are ruses which have no exit or are labyrinthine. Predating creatures will either find themselves in a closed or convoluted space and will have to withdraw, or if they are weaker than I they will become prey.

Although I have dug my burrow deep in the ground under tightly packed soil and moss, a keen-nosed creature will smell the carcasses I have stored in my keep and in several of the smaller units. That is a danger I have had to undertake because the weather gets cold, windy, and wet, and as I've suggested, I am not incapable, only less capable, of hunting above ground rather than trapping in my burrow.

Danger is how I have lived my life and even with the very good possibility of being savaged and swallowed by a stronger creature, I have few complaints. Living above ground in the melee of what is called civilization has never appealed to me.

True, living alone underground can get lonely, but I am an avid dreamer who imagines a world before the current world which was marked by a degree of civility and even sympathy for those less fortunate. Now, and for some time, the current world outside this burrow has become cruel, greedy, and degraded beyond measure.

In a word, deep sleep and savory freshly caught prey have more than made up for any loneliness I might suffer. Which is not to say that burrow living is without its problems. Because of intemperate weather, I have to constantly check on the fastness of my dozen units and especially my keep. Even as deep in the earth as I live it can get wet and the soil can become soft and susceptible to violent trespassing. Hence I make rounds every day to ensure that my units and keep are as tightly impermeable as I can make them. For these tasks I am naturally armless and so use my bony protrusive forehead to secure the walls of my units, routinely pounding until my forehead bleeds.

I cease pounding when the walls are sound and the units and high-vaulted keep are utterly silent. Because many creatures live undergound at several levels, a keen ear, such as I possess, will discern sounds which to other ears are unheard. These sounds are usually feint and in different registers, the higher register most often belonging to the smaller game. The sounds as you would expect are always rhythmic and nearly always I will trace the sounds to their source, which when I have a clear advantage I will pounce on and savage. Unless the sounds are produced by what are called small fry, tiny creatures not worth pursuing.

Where the sound emanates from a stronger creature than I, I will either tolerate it until it leaves or lure it outside the burrow by displaying a savory edible. If I cannot elude or subdue the predator no matter which of the dozen units it has inhabited, I will have to move my burrow. This would obviously amount to an extraordinary amount of work.

I have had several close calls over the years, but rather amazingly I have never had to move my burrow. Still I worry. How many times have I been woken out of a deep delicious sleep to the sound of a creature usually small but not always? Once, a brown bear, fresh from hibernation found itself in one of my units, but, happily, it was one of the deceptive units with no exit. I immediately moved outside the burrow with the pelt of a recently killed prey and lured the sleepy bear back outside into the brush.

You may wonder whether I ever considered teaming with a female creature of my own species. I haven't because my species is well-known for its opportunistic savaging of its own kind. I would be afraid to go to sleep and so would she. But do I miss having cubs or small fry to, so to speak, continue my name? No, I do not.

It is my opinion that the burrowless world has

genocided itself, and I do worry that the dying of the outside world will drive surviving humans underground, even as it will drive them underwater and into space.

My own termination is arriving soon, and the best I can wish for is that the human world somehow hangs on until after I am gone.

I have no regrets except having been born at all into a cruelly misguided human-centered world which has become untenable not just for humans but for every living thing. But since that is the fate of living things for reasons unclear despite the prophecies in the holy books, I cannot be displeased that I have lived my life underground with its fundamental ups and downs: chase, capture, cannibalism.

At one time while dreaming in the womb I actually imagined becoming a verbal or visual artist, but all I could foresee was conforming stupidity and mindless rejection

The one notable advantage of growing old as a preying creature is sleep, fine deep sleep, even with the prospect of being awakened suddenly by foreign sounds. When I was younger and much stronger those sounds stirred my spirit of adventure with their prospect of the chase and even battle to the death. That of course is no longer the case, which is the reason I have taken such pains with the construction of my burrow.

THE OCTOPUS

Threatens boundaries.

Its body, a boneless mass of soft tissue, has no fixed shape.

The largest species, the Giant Pacific, with an arm span of seven meters, weighing a hundred pounds, will fit through an opening an inch wide.

Combined with their remarkable strength—a mature Giant Pacific can lift thirty pounds with each of its 1600 suckers.

Octopuses are notoriously difficult to keep in captivity.

Octopuses have escaped their aquarium tanks through small holes or lifted the lid of their tanks, scuttling across stretches of dry land for five miles back home to the sea.

Octopuses do not possess a stable color or texture, changing at will to match their surroundings; a camouflaged octopus can be invisible from a few feet away.

Like humans, they have a central nervous system, except there is no sharp distinction between brain and body.

An octopus's neurons are dispersed throughout its body, with two-thirds of the neurons in its arms; each arm can act intelligently on its own, grasping, manipulating, hunting.

In evolutionary terms, octopus intelligence is an anomaly.

The last common ancestor between octopuses and humans was a primitive, blind worm-like creature six hundred million years ago.

Other creatures so evolutionarily distant from humans—lobsters, snails, slugs, clams—rate low cognitively.

Octopuses frustrate the evolutionary division between intelligent vertebrates and simple-minded invertebrates.

They are sophisticated problem solvers; they learn, use tools; and show a capacity for mimicry, deception, even humor.

Their extreme strangeness makes them hard to study.

Octopus intelligence is like and utterly unlike human intelligence.

WOLVERINE

The wandering male with stubby legs embodies all the elusive mustelid's personality traits when it trekked hundreds of miles from northwest Wyoming through desert and sagebrush to the Rocky Mountain National Park in central Colorado. There he spent a few years looking, unsuccessfully, for a mate, before turning back north, walking hundreds of more miles before getting shot by a ranch hand in North Dakota.

Wolverines live underground?
Yes.
Why was he shot?
Because he was wild.

LETTERS TO MILENA

In *Letters to Milena* I summarize Kafka's letters to Milena Jesenska, a gentile Czech from a prominent Prague family which, excluding Milena, was nationalist and (in the instance of her father) virulently anti-Semitic.

Milena was 23 when she translated Kafka's "The Stoker," from German to Czech, which she published in a Czech literary journal. "The Stoker" was to become the first chapter in Kafka's unpublished novel *Amerika*, which he wrote in German as he wrote all of his work.

Kafka was 36 and met Milena once in Vienna where she was living unhappily with her husband Ernst Pollak, a Jewish writer and literary critic. They spent parts of four affectionate days together, but with no consummation. They met again much later for a single difficult day in Gmund, a town between Austria and Czechoslovakia.

Milena asked that her letters be destroyed, so what we have here is a summary of Kafka's letters to Milena, including Milena's obituary of Kafka.

**

Prague, July 1920

At the public swimming pool I spit up something red. You will agree, Milena, that was unusual and interesting. I looked at it for a while and forgot it. Then it started occurring frequently, and generally whenever I wanted to I could spit out something red. At that point it had become boring.

Prague, July 1920 (Tuesday AM)

How tired you sound in your letter from Saturday. I won't say a thing, just seat you in the armchair (you claim you haven't done enough nice things for me, but is there any greater honor you can show me than simply allowing me to sit in front of you?) So now I seat you in the chair, unable to grasp the scope of my fortune with eyes hands and my poor heart, my happiness that you are here and really mine. In truth it is not at all you I love, but rather the existence you have bestowed on me.

Prague, July 1930

Between the daytime world and that "half hour in bed" you once wrote of with disdain, as if it were men's business, there is an abyss I cannot span.

To resort to black magic at night—hasty, panting, helpless, demonically possessed—in order to capture what every day gives freely to open eyes!

Maybe there isn't any other way to have children. Maybe children too are black magic. Look into my eyes, Milena.

Prague, July 1930

The grave is strange. I was looking for it, but too timidly, then I very boldly starting making bigger and bigger and then huge circles around it and finally mistook another grave for the right one.

I felt better in the cemetery than in the city. This good feeling lasted for a long time. I walked through the city as if it were a graveyard.

Why am I not, I wondered, the happy wardrobe in your room which has you in full view whenever you're sitting in your chair or when you are lying down or sleeping (all blessings upon your sleep, Milena).

Prague, July 1920 (Thursday)

Am I really kind and patient? I don't know about that, but I do know that your telegram does the whole body good, so to speak. Still, it's just a telegram, not a proffered hand.

Last night I committed a murder for your sake, Milena. A wild dream, a bad, bad night. Perhaps it isn't love when I say you are what I love the most—you are the knife I turn inside myself.

Prague, July 1920 (Tuesday evening)

All day I did nothing. Or else listened to a very light pain working in the temples. All day long I was preoccupied with your letters, in agony, in love, in worry, and in an entirely indefinite feat of the indefinite, which is indefinite because it is infinitely beyond my strength. I didn't dare read your letter a second time, and there is one half-page I didn't dare read at all.

Why can't one accept the fact that the right thing to do is live inside this very special tension which keeps suicide suspended?

Prague, July 1920

I am dirty, Milena, infinitely dirty, which is why I go on so much about purity. No one sings as purely as those who inhabit the deepest hell.

Grimmenstein, August 1920

I can't say I am very well prepared for your birthday, Dear Milena, having slept worse than usual, with my head hot, my eyes burned out, my temples causing me torment, and my cough. I don't think I can offer congratulations of any length without coughing. Fortunately, no congratulations are necessary, just a thank you for being on this earth. As you can see, I am at the sanatorium in Grimmenstein. Max took me here early in the AM.

Grimmenstein, August 1920 (Tuesday dawn)

I'm not saying goodbye, Milena. There isn't any goodbye, unless gravity, which is lying in wait for me, pulls me down entirely. But how could it, since you are alive.

You cannot, Milena, exactly understand what

it's about. I don't understand it myself. I am shaking from the eruption; you can torture me to the point of insanity, but what it is and what it ultimately wants I do not know. I only know what it wants at the moment: quiet, darkness, crawling off somewhere, and I must obey, there is no other choice.

Grimmenstein September 1920

I haven't had the heart to read your letters. You ask about my weight; it is very low—57.967 kgs. The "nurse" is watching my hand tremble as I write. She won't leave. And you say you have blood coming out of your mouth. Much as I loathe them for my own sake, you must see a doctor, Milena.

Prague, September 1920

Back in my flat and back to work. The cough has stopped, though not completely, but I am grateful. I am grateful too that you have stopped spitting blood even though you did not see the doctor.

How is it, dear Milena, that you are not afraid of me or disgusted by me?

Prague, September 1920

Few things are certain, but one is that we'll never live together, share a flat, body to body, at a common table.

You say the thought of death makes you anxious. Of course. I'm just terribly afraid of pain. That's bad. To want death but not pain is a bad sign. Otherwise one can risk death. One has simply been sent out as a biblical dove, and having found nothing green, now slips back into the darkness of the ark.

Prague, October 1920

No, Milena, we don't have the shared possibility we thought we had in Vienna.

We didn't have it then either. But the fact that you chose to translate precisely this passage is a sign we have similar tastes. Yes, torture is extremely important to me—my sole occupation is being tortured.

Prague, Mid-October 1920

I've been spending every afternoon on the streets wallowing in anti-Semitic hate. Yesterday I heard someone calls the Jews a "mangy race," to wild applause and laughter.

I just looked out the window: mounted police with fixed bayonets, a screaming mob dispersing, and up here in the window the unsavory shame of living under constant protection.

Prague, November 1920

Two letters arrived today. I'm so ashamed of my letters I scarcely dare open your replies. I keep trying to convey something which cannot be conveyed, to explain something which cannot be explained, something in my bones. Not you, Milena, only I am at fault, because there was too little truth, lies told out of fear of myself and fear of people. Lying is horrible, there's no worse mental agony. I beg you to let me be silent.

June 1, 1924.

Milena Jesenska's obituary for Franz Kafka

Dr. Franz Kafka, a German writer who lived in Prague, died in the Kierling Sanatorium, near Klosterneuburg bei Vien. Few people knew him in Prague, for he was a recluse, in dread of life. He had been suffering from a lung disease for years, and although he worked to cure it, he also consciously nourished it, and fostered it in his thoughts. He once wrote in a letter: When heart and soul can't bear it any longer, the lung takes on half the burden, so that the grief is distributed more evenly.

His disease lent him a miraculous tenderness and an almost horribly uncompromising intellectual refinement. Physically, Franz Kafka loaded his entire intellectual fear of life onto the shoulders of his disease. He was shy, anxious, meek, and kind, yet the books he wrote are gruesome and painful.

He saw the world as full of invisible demons tearing apart and destroying defenseless humans.

He was too clairvoyant, too intelligent to be capable of living, and too weak to fight. He was weak the way noble, beautiful people are, incapable of struggling against their fear of misunderstanding, malice, or intellectual deceit, and because they recognize their own helplessness in advance, their submission only shames the victor.

He has written the most significant books of modern German literature, books that are true, stark, and painful. They are full of dry scorn and the sensitive perspective of a prophet who saw the world so clearly that he couldn't bear it, a man bound to die since he refused to make concessions or take refuge as others do in fallacies of reason, or the unconscious.

BLACK /WHITE

A white male sits in the pilot seat of a late-model SUV.

The car has as many electronic gewgaws as a jet fighter.

The kind of aircraft the US is giving to the Ukraine in the US's proxy war against Russia.

The "white" male is Jewish hence not white in the eyes of the neo-Nazis and the extreme Right who are suddenly everywhere.

However, the Jewish male is precisely white in the eyes of the #MeToo armies which are ubiquitous and ever vigilant, and since he is, he has always thought, heterosexual, he must watch his step.

Because the male has written critically of Israel's violence against Palestinians, he is filthily anti-Jewish in the eyes of the Israeli parliament as well as most Israeli citizens and Jews worldwide.

In a word, he can't comfortably drive his preposterously complex car and must be extremely vigilant when consorting with females or making comments about Israel apartheid or "seeming" Jewish in the exponentially multiplied enclaves of far right hatred.

He writes books—did I say that? He writes what he calls docufiction, but because he is Jewish and not Jewish, white and not white, heterosexual and nervous, what are his options?

VESPERS

There was a time when I went to vespers nearly every evening, not out of devotion but for the sight of a slender girl with long, shapely legs. The church was sparsely attended at that hour, comprised mostly of older women, so I tried to get as close to the girl as I could without being too obvious. She looked to be perhaps 17 with glossy black hair which she fastened in a bun, but once, before the service began, I notice her shaking her hair out in order to bind it, and it reached to the small of her back. Her facial features were delicate and her entire bearing was shy, reserved. She recited the hymns softly and sang equally softly with what appeared to be a mezzo or possibly contralto voice.

Though I was young, tall and not unattractive, I was new in the city and cautious about new acquaintances, including beautiful young women; perhaps especially beautiful young women. In a word I was satisfied merely sitting behind the young woman and smelling the faint lemony scent that wafted from her hair as she turned her head in song.

One vespers when for unclear reasons I was especially looking forward to observing my "paramour," she didn't attend.

With the service already begun, it was unseemly to leave, so I went through the motions while observing the supplicants in the sparsely filled church. One person caught my eye; he was in the second row farthest from me and he was behaving strangely. He was stretched out over several pews on his stomach and was reciting the psalms and singing the canticles very loudly, even shouting out some phrases. Between these outbursts he would bang his head forcefully on the pew in front of him. Then he would glance around to make certain the other congregants saw what he was doing. He was an exhibitionist of a very low order and I made up my mind to let him know how he was behaving.

I tried to get to him after that first display, but he must have noticed my close observance and managed to slip through a door behind the pulpit. The following eve I had other obligations and didn't attend vespers. But the evening after I was free and especially looking forward to seeing and inhaling the lovely congregant.

You can imagine my frustration when, again, she didn't appear. And by the time I recorded her absence the service had begun and it was too late for me to leave. I had actually forgotten the disturbed young man until I saw him again in the second row lying prone over several pews and already making odd hooting sounds and looking around as though for approval, though the service had not formally begun.

With my eyes trained on him exclusively, he was even more obnoxious than before, banging the front of the pew with his shoe—or maybe it was some object from his pocket. When he gazed around the church for approval his eyes appeared to evade mine. It seemed clear he had not forgotten that first episode, but this time I would keep an eye on the door behind the pulpit. Meanwhile, most of the handful of other congregants did not seem to take notice of the fellow's outbursts. They were evidently used to it. I wasn't, and I planned to have it out with him.

Well, he eluded me again. One of the elderly congregants initiated a conversation with me that I couldn't evade. As I was absently nodding my head the disturbed fellow had slipped away.

While bicycling to my flat I made up my mind to stay away from vespers—maybe for good; after not seeing the lovely girl for nearly a week, it seemed likely that she had ceased to "worship" at that church. On the other hand the disturbed young man would surely be there indulging in his manic outbursts.

Despite my resolution, after four days I returned to vespers and both the young beauty and the disturbed fellow were present. Curiously, the young man had spread himself out on the very pew behind the girl on which I had sat. I am sure he did this intentionally, and I was forced to sit several rows back on the left aisle, much farther away from the girl than previously. That enraged me and when the service ended I waited outside between the main and side exits.

Again he exited through the pulpit door but I was prepared and grabbed hold of him by the shoulder, which was very thin, even child-like. I steered him into a narrow side street and sat him down on a stone bench. He gazed at me with frightened, almost delirious eyes.

"What do you think you're doing?" I put it to him with one hand still holding his thin shoulder.

"Oh, sir, please don't be unhappy with me," he cried out. "I can't help what I do."

His voice was deeper than I expected, and his face and bone structure were almost handsome. He gazed at me only briefly then bent his head and seemed to close his eyes. I thought he might be crying.

I said: "You howl and scream and then look around the church for approval. Why do you do that?"

He looked over my shoulder. "I can't help it. I must be recognized—"

"Recognized by elderly ladies in their pews?"

"Recognized by anyone—or else I die."

"Die?"

"Yes, my friend. Die."

I removed my grip from his shoulder.

"When I gaze about me," he continued, now almost whispering, "all I see are cruelty and acquisition. Erecting, constructing, traffic, monster trucks, coursing like contaminated blood through my veins."

He looked down at the graffiti on the broken cement ground and whispered intensely: "And what about the poor, the abject, the tormented on the streets and in the churches, like me—and you?"

"Me," I repeated. "What do you know of me?"

Now he turned his bony handsome face to me with a faint ironic expression.

I said: "The complaints about the failing world and its miseries are familiar to many of us, and that, you say, is why you behave the way you do in church."

"I didn't say that," he replied firmly.

"What is your name?" I enquired in a softer tone.

"K," he responded. "My name is K. Same as you."

"What do you mean?" I said, suddenly alarmed.

"Isn't your name Joseph K?" he demanded.

"Yes, it is," I admitted.

"And haven't you been coming to vespers to get close to the beautiful girl?"

I looked at him without responding.

"To gaze at her and smell the faint sweet scent from her hair?

I continued to look at him, though my eyes had become blurry as though partially awaking out of a dream.

"She is my sister, you know."

"Your sister?"

Looking at his face more attentively I actually noted a resemblance to the girl.

"Exactly, Mr K," and both she and I are fully aware that you have been glaring at her with an eye to abuse her."

"Abuse her!" I protested. "What do you mean?"

"My sister's name is K, as well, and she and I have been considering notifying the police."

"What are you talking about?"

"I think you know what we are talking about. You are a lonely man, Joseph K. Isolated, living alone in a strange city. You are starving for tenderness; at the same time you lack the courage—or is it grace?—to make a move. My sister sees this. She—and I too—feel sorry for you. At the same time we can see in your eyes that you are dangerous, not to be trusted."

"My eyes?"

"Yes, your eyes, Mr. K. You have the eyes of a wild animal—a jackal, perhaps—that has gotten displaced in this unbearable world."

My mind turned suddenly to the jackal, trying to

remember how it looked.

"We know full well that you wish to assault her."

"Abuse her! Now assault her! How?" I asked.

"Do I have to spell it out, Mr Joseph K?

Silence.

"What do you mean to do, K?" I asked.

He responded at once with a certain authority: "My sister and I want you to refrain from visiting vespers at once or we will lodge our complaint with the Politzei."

"Your complaint is what? That I abused her with violent intent?"

"Exactly," he responded firmly.

With that, he gave me an authoritative look, got up and hastened away.

.

BUTCHER LOVE

Gansevoort Street meat district, Greenwich Village North.

Slaughtered stock animals hang from their hooves.

Butchers in bloody aprons, blood beneath their fingernails, blood on their teeth, on their thick shoes. And Kafka whose grandfather on his father's side was a butcher.

Nouvelle merde justly describes the SM dungeon club recently opened in the meat district on Gansevoort Street.

Want to enter the SM joint?

Pony up $100, fems admitted without charge.

Indeterminate genders?

You'll need to check with management.

The club opens at midnight, goes deep into the dawn hours.

My invite comes from a friend of a friend of a friend who works for Disney.

This isn't well-known: A Disney "affiliate" reportedly owns the club and sister clubs in Soho, Chelsea, and upper Broadway just north of Columbia University. just south of Harlem.

Is there still a "Harlem"?

Didn't Columbia University buy up Harlem and evict the tenants?

This is off the record.

The Disney affiliate insists the Harlem tenants weren't tenants, they were welfare cheats, freeloaders, crackheads, crazy-haired rappers.

So yeah, the evicted were black. What can I tell you?

The club is called Genet, as in Jean Genet.

Homo-masochist, prideful petty thief, celebrated anti-saint, prize-winning author.

Genet claimed to have read and admired Kafka in French translation.

Disney (affiliate) SM clubs include Genet 1, Genet 2, Genet 3, Genet 4.

The joint in the meat district on Gansevoort is Genet 2.

Raunchy dungeon ambiance.

Up to the nano body-in-pain participants.

Hardened stock animal blood on the concrete floor.

It is a stormy Monday, 3:30 AM, but G-2 is rocking.

They call it stormy Monday but Tuesday's just as bad.
Wednesday's worse and Thursday's oh so sad.
The eagle flies on Friday.

Maybe, but it's still Monday early dawn in G-2 on Gansevoort.

Naked males crawling on the concrete, whimpering, knees and elbows bloody.

Dominatrices with whips and paddles, electric prods.

Human—and possibly humanoid—clusters in various stages of undress groping.

Above the concrete "arena" on three sides are wooden bleachers; I'm sitting in one.

The designer-rough arena resembles a much larger version of an MMA "cage."

Mixed Martial Arts.

You've seen it on TV between commercials.

Steroidal young men with shaved heads, florid tats, and cauliflower ears manically grappling and kicking.

The grapplers come from everywhere, including Central and Eastern Europe.

Which brings us back to Kafka.

K weighed about 57 kilos (125 lbs), he remarked in his letters.

K was Jewish of course, and though born in Prague wrote in German and lived in Berlin and Austria during the Weimar period.

Most of the meat outlets on Gansevoort label themselves kosher.

PETA reports that a kosher slaughterhouse in Chicago produced at least "300 instances of inhumane slaughter, in which fully conscious cows, hung upside-down, had their sensitive muzzles shocked with electric prods, had their tracheas and esophagi ripped from their throats with meat hooks or knives, as they writhed in pools of their own blood, moaning, trying desperately to stand for up to three minutes as blood streamed from their throats."

Here in G-2, I'm strictly an observer, and one scene stays with me.

A middle-aged couple is sitting in the bleachers above me holding hands when the male, thin / pale, separates himself, descends into the arena, removes his clothes, is bound to a pole and flogged by an extremely tall masked dominatrix in ebony latex with a cat o' nine tails.

I see the sardonic gleaming smile beneath the mask.

She flogs him mercilessly on the lower back, buttocks, thighs . . .

He whimpers.

Stock animals whimper.

They shriek in pain.

Dolphins shriek in pain in a register we cannot hear.

So do rabbits, commonly ignored by humans.

So do very small animals and amphibians.

The injured goldfinch I'm cupping in my hands.

Tune in, turn on, hear them scream, shriek, whimper.

The pale male whimpers and screams, he bleeds from his thighs and buttocks.

It looks like blood.

I glance up at the woman, his other half.

She observes without expression.

After a delirious 15 minutes he is released.

And now I smell shit, vaguely.

Could be a participant's cologne.

Or savory remnant of slaughtered stock animals.

The calf, dead, released finally into the suffering animal afterworld.

Infinitely above humankind.

I am impressed that the pale male, bleeding, naked, dragging his clothes, is embraced tenderly by his female companion.

He broadcasts his "weakness," whimpers like a tormented calf, shrieks like a laboratory rabbit, and the woman (she wears sunglasses, I can't see her eyes) kisses him tenderly, sensually on the mouth.

Kafka broadcasts his weakness and his fearful desire to be touched tenderly, and his lover takes him in. Perfect! But is the whole SM club-love a fantasy?

When a friend, in "real time," asks how he is feeling, K says: "I consider it a good day when I can stand in the corner and breathe."

GOD DID IT

A 42-year-old homeless man believed to be linked to two feces attacks is in custody.

A woman had feces violently shoved down her pants and another woman was smeared with feces.

Police said a homeless person was behind this week's attacks and that the women did not know their attacker.

The man, discovered in a junkyard in downtown Brooklyn, was identified as Double X, homeless.

His comment when he viewed the video of his feces-in-shorts assault was *God did it.*

GITMO

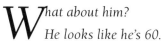*hat about him?*
He looks like he's 60.

He's 25, maybe 30.
Snatched off the street in Baghdad when he was 9.

Charge?

Terrorism.

Never represented by counsel?

No.

Tortured?

Yes.
The Abu Ghraib routine.

Did he confess to any crime?

No.

Why is he still held?

The Biden administration has changed the name from Guantanamo to Camp Justice. Evidently, justice has still not been served.

Camp Justice!

Right.
I'm UN as you know and have been here just 5 and a half months.
Everything I say is off the record, remember.

What about him?

He's 35, been in Gitmo since he was 12.
Yemeni, plucked off the streets in Sanaa.

Yemeni! The US wasn't at war with Yemen.

Saudi Arabia was and is.

The US was backing Saudi and still is.

The US and Israel's grand enemy Iran has been arming Yemen.

So they tortured the Yemeni boy without counsel.
What did they expect to get out of him?

Nothing.

That's how the US black sites function.

Torture, no counsel, bunch of years in isolation.

It's a ritual, unquestioned by any entity that cares or has the power to intervene.

This man—why is he caged?

Iraqi. One of five defendants accused of taking part in the 9/11 bombings.

He's been diagnosed with PTSD with secondary psychosis linked to his abuse during his 20-plus years in CIA custody. He never confessed to the 9/11 accusation, and there's good reason to believe he wasn't involved.

[pause]

What about Cuba?
What *about* Cuba?

Fidel was alive when Guantanamo started operating.
He had to know what was going on in his own country.

He knew.

When Khrushchev backed down after JFK's nuclear threat back in '62 Fidel accepted that he had to give up Gitmo to the Yanks.

Realpolitik.

So how come it took the UN this long to make a move?
And what does the UN expect to achieve?

At a minimum we hope to get these illegal prisoners released.

First in Gitmo, then in black sites elsewhere around the world.

How many black sites are there?

We don't know for certain.

At least 60 we expect.

Biden and his people know about them?

Biden knows but probably forgets he knows.

His people know, of course.

Not that they would admit it.

And you understand that the UN can only do so much.

If for example a country like Turkey or Indonesia or Bulgaria refuses us access or denies they have black sites—which we know or assume they have—we are scarcely in position to force the issue.

And if you publicize this—the black sites madness—in the US?

You know the response to that.

Americans have other things on their minds.

You see how they respond to migrants uprooted by wars not of their making, wars in which the US often played a leading role.

What then are we left with?

The UN can do no more than advise.
It doesn't have the capacity to enforce.
That is what we are left with.

NINE SONS

I have nine sons and I will appraise them in no particular order.

My **first son** is shy and reticent, like his father, people say. But I do not feel that sort of affinity with him. The primary reason is he is a materialist; he will spend half a day balancing his checkbook and seeming to take the greatest delight in it, even though he does not have a large amount of money (at least to my knowledge). Similarly, he will spend four or five hours on his laptop pursuing an algorithm in every minuscule detail to end up—where? Nowhere that I can determine. But his eyes shine as though he has unearthed a vein of gold, that shining metal that leads men—especially white men, as Crazy Horse has it—astray. This son is routinely polite to his father and siblings but never not distracted. He is a slight young man, with fine blond hair and regular features which other humans often find appealing, except that he does not bear scrutiny. He seems to lack even the remotest sense of physical *amour-propre*.

My **second son** is the polar opposite of my first son, at least physically. He is tall and gracefully athletic. Whatever sport or game is being played will interest him and he will become proficient, even expert at the game rapidly and seemingly effortlessly. I say the sport will interest him, but only so long as he becomes proficient in it. Then he will drop it and turn his attention elsewhere which for him is money. Every investment opportunity or speculation which seems promising will seize his attention and he will invest what money he has at the moment in the opportunity. But it will never bear fruition. He will invariably lose his money and be in the degrading position of having to borrow to discharge his debt and invest further. But the further investment will also fail and yet he will never cease attempting, accruing numerous debts in the process. As his father, I've tried to reason with him, but to no effect. As elegantly proficient as he is in sport, he is that unlucky in the ruthless sport of money accumulation.

In **my third son** what you see is what you get. He is slender with a smooth olive complexion, and what is called romantic features. Thick wavy black hair, "sultry" black eyes, a short straight nose, full lips, a cleft chin, and small ears close to his head. The opposite and even the same sex seem to find him eminently desirable and nearly all of his time is spent romancing in the homes or flats of his paramours. He wears simple elegant clothes which his paramours often purchase for him, and everything he wears looks as if it were tailored for his body exclusively. He goes to sleep very late and gets up correspondingly late in the AM, but he always looks fresh, shining, ready for romance. When we talk at all it is to exchange amiable meaningless words after 2 AM.

My **fourth son** is a lonely young man. Intelligent and artistic, he is especially adept at painting extreme closeups of flowers from the live which he will customarily buy at a florist shop or nursery. Occasionally he will even model his flower on a painted image—one of Georgia O'Keeffe's for example. I say he is lonely, yet he is always among people—friends, relatives, his siblings. He sets his small easel and model flower in a space with people—the more the better. And their chatter seems to complement his artistic imagination. He is and aspires to be nothing more than an amateur painter, and when he is not at his art he is with people—the more the better. In the company of people my fourth son is eminently satisfied to listen and nod his head.

My **fifth son**, deliberately buried here among his siblings, is my brutal father reborn. Broad-shouldered with ramrod posture and a military mustache, we scarcely communicate with each other, and when we do he responds critically in word or gesture to anything I say, no matter how trivial. On the rare occasions when the sons, or most of them, and their father sit for dinner, he—my fatherly son—assumes the lead and often as not manages to praise the authoritarian anti-Semites of Prague. Like them, this son speaks in German, never in Czech, and when he comes to table or leaves rarely neglects to click his heels like an officer of the Kaiser's imperial guard. For all that, he is lazy, refusing to work at what he calls "menial" jobs, and so spends his time going to young fascist meetings. He is 19 years old and the best I can do is wait two more years, when he is of age to send him out on his own.

Despite what appear to be notable differences in appearance and inclination in my sons, they each bear a physical likeness—however remote—one to the other and each to their father. None of this applies to my **sixth son**. Physically, he is a giant, six feet 11 inches, and he has been pursued by agents and other gold-sniffing parasites of the professional basketball league (NBA) since he was in the third grade, when he was already nearly six feet tall. You may think that at his extraordinary height he is awkward; the opposite is true. He was and always has been a confident giant, quiet, dexterous, surprisingly quick in his movements, a wonderful athlete without any trace of Acromegaly or Gigantism He is now 22 and after spending a single year at UCLA is the starting center of the Los Angeles Clippers and earning many millions of dollars. He lives in Malibu with his girlfriend, a professional tennis player currently ranked 4th in the globe.

My **seventh son** began as a cinephile loving old movies, current films, videos, virtually anything on a screen and in motion. Now, logically enough, he is a professional film maker; that is, he is a film director who at age 29 has already directed four films which have elicited virtually uniform praise from film critics. I call them "films" because I have always been an "art film" buff. My son and his admirers call them movies which is doubtless a more precise designation. They are all rather quick-moving offbeat comedies which are not easy to describe. One is about a pancake house that is in wacky competition with other pancake houses. Another features a very small—even dwarfish—albino Sikh (Sikhs originally come from the Punjab in northwestern India) who speaks multiple languages and can slide effortlessly from one language to the other. He is also a stand-up comic who tells raunchy jokes in a dozen languages and has the off-putting tendency to laugh at his own jokes. Except that in the gifted Sikh's routine the laughing at his own jokes is usually charming. I won't describe my movie director son's other two films here.

Different as one son is from the other, the most radically different from his siblings is my **eighth son** who, though 28-years-old, is and has been since a child a compassionate human of the highest order—if I can put it that way. Compassion is a concept that has lost its footprint in our dying globe, but not for my son. When I think of him I think of Mother Teresa or Cesar Chavez, or even Mahatma Gandhi. As an adolescent he volunteered to help charities feed the unfortunate at Thanksgiving and Christmas, doling out food behind the counter in long queues of feeding stations throughout the city's underbelly. What money he made from his job of stacking books and videos at a local library he spent on hand-to-hand charities, such as going to homeless encampments and handing out 5-dollar bills or giving what money he had to animal shelters that home abandoned domestic animals. You observe that I speak of my eighth son in the past tense because he died after traveling to the Palestinian West Bank to be of use to the mistreated people there. Specifically, he was murdered when he put his body between an Israeli bulldozer sweeping away Palestinian homes and a ten-year-old boy throwing rocks at the bulldozer. The bulldozer was closely followed by IDF tanks. Both my son and the boy were shot dead by the tank's 120 mm gun. Nor did the Israeli government permit my family to claim and cremate what remained of his body.

My **ninth son** is the youngest and easily the most *au courant* of his siblings. He listens to rap music, knows the artists, and can recite the lyrics. Though nominally male he commonly wears makeup and nail polish. He is involved with pronouns and refuses to be called either male or female, gay or straight. He has many young friends, nearly all of them like "him" of indeterminate gender and sometimes contentious when an outsider makes a "political" error. My son (as I call him for the sake of symmetry) is well-built and copiously tattooed on his left arm and left leg. The ever evolving acronym: **LGBTQA+** is prominent on his muscular left thigh. After community college he moved from job to job, ending up at Starbucks, where surprisingly he has become militantly union-oriented, is in fact president of the local Starbucks union. He rarely sleeps at home. In our most recent brief exchange I wished him luck in the ongoing union fight against Starbucks.

BLOOD DONOR

Hello, I'd like to donate blood.

Whose blood?

My blood.

Did you consult our website?

Yes. It recommended phoning.

We sell ammo. Ammunition for handguns.

If you possess a handgun, especially a semi-automatic, you know how hard it is to find ammo.

We sell ammo at highly competitive prices.

Where do you live?

Mission Hills.

That's only ten minutes from us.

Twelve minutes max.

You know where Kearney Mesa is?

Vaguely.

I don't want to buy ammo.

I want to donate my blood.

You say you don't possess a gun of any kind?

No.

That's a mistake, if you don't mind me saying.

It's a jungle out there.

If you want a semi-automatic, most amateurs like Glocks—they are lightweight but very powerful.

We also recommend revolvers, short-barrel .38s especially for amateurs.

AGAIN

Hello, I'd like to donate blood.

Did you consult our website?

Yes. It sent me here.

What is your blood type?

AB.

Are you a healthy individual?

No recent surgeries or atypical blood loss?

How old are you?

I am 46 and healthy.

No recent surgeries or atypical blood loss.

Why do you want to donate your blood?

Because of the massive violence, people killing each other in the streets.

Because of the extreme climate crisis, people becoming sick from inhaling smoke from wildfires while the temperature is routinely plus-100.

As a result, people—especially children and the elderly—collapsing, even dying in the streets.

We don't pay for blood donations.

 I know.

Sorry. I will have to put you on a brief hold.

Nine minutes later

Sorry. What did you say your name was?

Kafka.

And your blood type is O.

AB. My blood type is AB.

I have to put you on a brief hold.

12 minutes later

Sorry about that, Mr . . .

Kafka. I would like to donate my blood which is type AB.

You've consulted our website?

Yes. It says that that type AB is needed.

Let me check Can you hold?

6 and a half minutes later.

Sorry. We have as much type AB as we can use. We are especially looking for A, B, and O.

AGAIN

Hello, I'd like to donate blood.
Did you consult our website?
Yes.
Hold on for a sec.

8 minutes later.

Sorry, we only accept blood donors via our website.

AGAIN

Hello, I'd like to donate my blood.
I am type AB.
I am 46 years old and healthy with no surgeries or atypical blood loss.
Did you consult our website?

Yes.

You understand that we do not pay for blood.

Yes, I understand that.

Can you provide a birth certificate or other ID with photo?

Yes, a driver's license.

You said you were 44?

46.

Our policy is that anyone wanting to provide blood who is over 45 must provide a note from their physician.

With letterhead.

It can also be sent online as an email or attachment.

Why?

To prove you are a healthy individual.

It is all detailed on our website.

Sorry, I will have to put you on a brief hold.

ELVES

Though of German origin, the belief that elves would function like incubi, pressing down on the sleeper's chest to cause frightful dreams, was and is widespread in Europe.

My parents were European immigrants and I have had "frightful dreams" my entire life. After I awake shouting and kicking, I welcome the dreams, frightful as they may be.

No life on earth
Can be hid from our dreaming

INCEL

D o you know what Incel means?

Well . . .

Involuntary celibate.
You know what that means?

Well . . .

Let's cut to the chase.
You battered her on the breasts and sent her to the emergency room.
You know that, correct?

No.
She hit me in the ear first with a 10-pound dumbbell.
She's a large person.
She lifts weights and so do I which is how this happened in the fitness place.

We were both trying to get a dumbbell from the rack
when she swung the ten pounder and hit me in the ear.
I simply pushed her away.

You know what the fitness place is called, correct?

All Gender . . .

All Gender Fitness Emporium.
You are a hetero male, correct?

What do you mean? Heterosexual? Yes.

You battered her on her breasts.
You know that, correct?

Look at my swollen face.
I can hardly talk.
She hit me with a dumbbell on my ear.

Before you said eye.

I never said eye.

She's in the emergency room, okay?

Why am I not in the emergency room?
You can see how my face is badly swollen.

You'll be in a padded cell if you don't answer my questions.
Do you have a girlfriend?

What?

Do you have a girlfriend?

I have a female friend.

Do you have sex with her?

No.

Why not?
Can't you get it up?

Человека

She is not my wife.
I am not a married man.
I see.

What's this all about?

It's about battery and sexual abuse.
You battered her breasts, okay?

She swung at me with a 10-pound dumbbell and hit me in the ear when we were both moving toward the dumbbell rack.
I simply pushed her away from me.

That isn't her narrative.
And it isn't the narrative of the woman who she was working out with.
Do you have anyone to corroborate your version?

I . . . don't know.
It was only the third time I've worked out there.
I am new in this city.

That woman you battered plans to press charges against you.

And like I said, she has a corroborating witness.

Do you have an attorney?

I don't—

Your name is Muhammad, right?

OBIT

You crouched at the womb sewing a shroud for the
  journey.

    Immediately you pricked yourself with the needle.

    Somehow you embarked left foot first.

    Thus began your long romance with female feet.

    The sole thing you share with Quentin Tarantino.

Once out you got lost at once.

(Had you stayed lost literature would never have
deviated)

    You found your way back / that became a motif.

    Get lost find your way back.

    Still you never quite knew where you were.

    Except in dream.

    Wasn't all of it dream?

    Even that compelled unspeakable: *writing*?

    Dreaming what you write or the other way around.

You dreamed they were leading you to the gas.

    Prophetic—it was early Weimar.

    Somehow you survived.

It may have been the dream that survived.

The gas never left you.

You dreamed you were one of the 36.

Out of the Jewish mystical books.

36 just men none knowing the others.

On their thin shoulders this defective planet resides.

Not resides, totters.

Were one just man to die he would be replaced at once.

Or else the entire edifice collapses.

The entire edifice <u>has</u> collapsed but that's a different "narrative."

It is the same narrative except told in dream.

Agonizing dream / without the agony you wouldn't write.

Without writing you wouldn't dream / would that matter?

No, it wouldn't matter, you think.

Feel don't think!

Aren't Jews feelers?

Those who aren't feckless / Aren't "good" at money.

Feelers & thinkers, often solemn, as often comical.

Walter Benjamin comes to mind and Marx—Karl & Groucho—autistic Einstein too. Kafka quintessentially.

Yourself, you've never balanced a checkbook.

Depending on providence which otherwise has not been kind.

As a child you were pretty, delicate.

Kids picked up on the delicate and bullied you.

You were different from normal kids.

Another ongoing motif.

You were too different not to be alone, which pained you.

Not being different meant being normal, which pained you.

Being alone was more painful than being normal / sometimes.

Then you became an athlete which made it easy to impersonate normal.

Until you lost spontaneity, watched yourself.

Watched yourself watching yourself.

Like Chekhov, Dostoyevsky.
Kafka too, especially his Hunger Artist.
(Your Russian-Jewish descendants)

Ah, then came girls.

Playing footsie with Kerrie, your 7th grade classmate under the desks.

You can see her slender feet now / smell the young girl feet-smell now.

You were four when Laraine, your adolescent cousin, napped in your parents' bed in her white bobby sox.

Tall, **imperially** slim, you liked displaying yourself.

Playing footsie and displaying yourself are not fucking and at that you became characteristically self-conscious.

Multiple ventures in multiple countries and nearly each a challenge / Nerves.

Remember what mad, brilliant Reich wrote on orgasm, you'd repeat to yourself.

The world is not your mother, you would repeat to yourself.

Urban infant, you taught yourself Nature.

Birds, trees, mammals, the nomenclature.

How to continue in all this made misery without proximity to creatures and trees!

Can't go on / Must go on.

Why must you? Bear witness—write.

& what a fucking pipe dream that turned out to be.

Drowning won't work because of your claustrophobia.

Hanging won't work for the same reason.

Crashing your car or jumping from a high place might injure others.

You can jump from a bridge into deep dusky water, if you're able to work your way to the jumping point.

Cutting your wrists (vertically not horizontally) is far from fail-safe.

A single cyanide capsule (Nazi Field Marshal Göring) would do it, if you can lay your hands on one.

Self-immolation like the American protestors against the US war on Vietnam.

Inadvertent electrocution—such as happened to

Thomas Merton in Thailand?

But how to maneuver the zig-zag lightning bolt into liking you?

Shoot yourself in the head or mouth with a small caliber pistol;

Small caliber because you don't want to leave too much of a mess.

If you shoot yourself in the chest use a shotgun.

But where do you get the hardware?

Texas, Florida, Arizona, Oklahoma, Idaho, Eastern Washington, Colorado . . .

In any *event, you are the invisible man rowing away from us.*

Kafka liked to row and was surprisingly good at it, but is it he?

All we can see are the oars in the small wooden boat rowing slowly toward the farthest border.

OBSERVATIONS & ANOMALIES

Set your body between the tank and the child throwing rocks; be shot to shreds along with the child. The bulldozer trailing the tank then buries the shreds in the broken ground along with the hut which houses a family of 9. (This is not the Zionism, K, that enthralled your friend and biographer, Max Brod).

**

Martyr has always signified great pain but was sometimes exemplary—it engendered further bravery. Now it signifies great pain and has been rendered invisible.

**

My brain is on fire while I am awake, and it is on fire when I sleep. What do I do?

**

Max Brod: "Kafka's language is fire but it leaves no soot behind."

**

You are old but still believe in the loving embrace. What do you do in this irremediably depersonalized culture? You locate an avatar; they are everywhere on social media.

**

K: "I love her as far as I am capable, but my love is buried almost to suffocation under fear and self-reproaches."

**

Much as I despise myself I cannot cease writing versions of myself in almost everything I write. Hence the "K" for the name of virtually every protagonist. If only K was a knight instead of a scribe.

**

K is anxious and so is the world and he feels (he thinks) more anxiety for the world than for himself.

**

Kafka claims the protuberance of his bony forehead

that blocks his way is the same bony forehead he uses as a battery ram to encase his "burrow" and deceive his enemies.

**

Max Brod writes: He was a wonderfully helpful friend. It was only in his own case that he was perplexed, helpless, an impression that owing to his self-controlled bearing, one did not get in personal contact with him except in rare, extreme cases.

**

Kafka liked to take long walks by himself with no fixed destination on Sundays thinking "Every day I wish myself off the earth."

**

Despite Max Brod's insistence that Kafka was a brilliant and amiable companion, the clear impression is that K was unsettled and fearfully articulate in human relations; that only in his written works was his extraordinariness evident.

**

Max Brod: Kafka was indifferent to fame. Writing for him, as he remarks in one of his journals, was "a form of prayer." That was Brod's justification, he says, for not destroying K writings as his friend instructed him to do.

**

Kafka was a deft artist with pen and ink, and his numerous self-portraits belie his grim written portraits; they display a jaunty image of himself with flexible long legs and a playful walking stick.

**

Czech Jews were outliers well before Weimar, and K's father was a proto-Nazi, Only Franz among his family of 6 recognized it but was spellbound before it.

**

Walter Benjamin, born 9 years after Kafka, was to Gershom Scholem, as Kafka was to Max Brod. Scholem, who emigrated to Israel, tried fruitlessly. to convince Benjamin to emigrate. A decade earlier Max

Brod tried without success to convince his close friend to follow him to Israel. Had they followed their friends to Israel, Kafka and Benjamin would have lived longer and written much less well.

**

"What I have to do l I have to do alone," Kafka said to Brod. "Become clear about the ultimate things. The Western Jew is not clear about them and therefore has no right to marry."

**

"The next morning Franz came to my office to see me. He had just been to the station to see F off. His face was pale, hard, and severe. But suddenly he began to weep."

**

Max Brod: Only once in his later years did I hear him refer his physical pain. He was lying in bed and when I asked how he was feeling he whispered: "It takes such a long time before one is crushed up quite small and squeezed through this last narrow hole."

**

Max Brod: "Kafka, like other great writers whose prose approximates musical speech, had no capacity for pure music. He once told me that he couldn't tell the difference between *The Merry Widow* and *Tristan and Isolde*."

**

Kafka died of consumption at age 41 in 1924. He didn't like to travel. Were he to have lived ten years longer the Nazi death camps would have claimed him.

HUNGER ARTIST

Well, the other shoe finally dropped.

Russia nuked Ukraine and US-led NATO nuked Russia.

Following their betters, India nuked Pakistan, North Korea nuked South Korea, and Israel nuked Iran.

Poisoned air, hurricanes, tsunamis, wildfires . . .

The US, separated by the contaminated Atlantic Ocean, was as yet un-nuked but was suffering from fires, radioactive fallout, and large parts of the country were experiencing nuclear winter.

Life, such as it was, sped on.

Moreover, politicians and their patron oligarchs, banding together, insisted that the poisoned atmosphere and billions dead amounted to a good thing because it would in effect end the migration of hyper-fertile brown and black humans thus serving as an impromptu population control.

To prevent "ordinary" Americans from thinking

critically or even clearly, the bread and circus mania slid into 8th gear. Sports, the mainstream "news" cycle, AI, and virtually every entertainment imaginable were everywhere online, streaming and "live" on TV.

K was an active participant in the Hunger Artists, humans who fasted to—or virtually to—death as entertainment.

The reasoning was that humans—those remaining on the dying planet—had enough of explosions and sirens and were eager to experience a, so to speak, softer dying.

Of course several of the hunger artists died of nuclear-related illnesses while others simply left the profession. K remained. In fact K came from an extended heritage of hunger artists, a number of whom had progeny fasters.

K had an agent—or impresario—who formerly represented MMA wrestlers and rugby players, many of whom were foreign and thus died outside the US in the nuclear blasts or their aftermath.

Hence the impresario moved to representing other entertainers, including hunger artists, but without enthusiasm. Obviously the hunger artist, though viewed and perhaps even acknowlwdged in certain quarters, did not bring in nearly the money that MMA fighters did.

Yes, even after two-thirds of the planet was destroyed beyond reclamation, money mattered as much as ever, possibly even more, for reasons not readily explicable.

Money did not matter to K. He lived alone, was childless, his needs were minimal. His interest was exclusively in his art.

After some maneuvering K's impresario got the hunger artist a half hour weekly late morning spot on ESPN2 between "mixed gender pickleball" and MMA reruns.

Pickleball can be loosely described as a combination of paddleball, badminton and ping-pong and because it was easy to play, encouraged all genders, and even made accommodation for the disabled, it was increasingly popular.

Initially the Hunger Artist was confused with the dystopian bloodsport Hunger Games. Other viewers found the hunger artist's art boring, comparing it to watching grass grow. But was a quiet meditative art such a bad thing with two-thirds of the world decimated and the final third in mortal distress?

The weekly half-hour was called "Q & A with the Hunger Artist."

K, 6-feet-tall, weighed 97 pounds, with his weight displayed on a large scale in lbs and kilos for the viewers. He wore sky blue pajamas, reclined in a grassy space with a peaceable expression on his ravaged face and responded to questions from viewers.

—*What do you eat or drink daily, K?*
I drink distilled water, nothing else.

—*Who is your hero faster, K?*
Mahatma Gandhi, without question.

His fasting, often close to death, helped drive the colonizing British out of India.

—*You seem to enjoy fasting. Is it the endorphins?*
Endorphins may have been a factor initially. But that was some time ago.

There is a long mostly unknown history of fasting of which I am a part.

—*Wouldn't you rather do something more masculine like kick-boxing?*
No, I am content doing what I'm doing.

—*Is your extreme fasting a religious art or a political maneuver like Gandhi?*
Gandhi's fasting was ethical more than political.
I consider my fasts a species of art, yes, but they are religious only if you wish them to be.

—*I bet you were bullied at school. Were you?*
Now and then. But I survived and here I am.

—*You weigh 97 pounds. How low do you think you can get without dying?*

If my health holds I think I can lose 25 more pounds.

—*Did you ever consider living a normal life, K? Getting married, having kids?*

Yes, I considered it and decided against it.

—*Someone who claims to know you said that you are compelled to be ascetic because of your purity and inability to compromise. Is that true?*

No.

—*Is there any food that you particularly miss, K?*

Strawberry ice cream.

—*What happens if you die, K?*

Then you won't have a weekly half-hour of Q & A with the Hunger Artist in the late morning on ESPN2.

**

K's weight got as low as 78 pounds when nuclear winter wiped out what remained of human (though not humanoid) civilization.

HAROLD JAFFE is the author of 30-plus novels, essays, short fiction, docufiction, and drama. His writings include *Porn-anti-Porn; Death Cafe; Induced Coma; 15 Serial Killers; Dos Indios; Anti-Twitter; Strange Fruit and Other plays; Jesus Coyote; Brando Bleeds; Madonna & Other Spectacles*; and *Beyond the Techno-Cave*. His work has been translated into French, Italian, German, Japanese, Turkish, and Serbo-Croatian.

Made in the USA
Columbia, SC
10 March 2024

32408529R00081